The Crooked Forest

Legacy of the Holey Stone

Joni Franks

Illustrated by: Ayin Visitacion

To order additional copies of this book, contact:
Xlibris
844-714-8691
www.Xlibris.com
Orders@Xlibris.com

ISBN:	Softcover	978-1-6641-7982-0
	Hardcover	978-1-6641-7983-7
	EBook	978-1-6641-7981-3

Library of Congress Control Number: 2021911997

Print information available on the last page

Rev. date: 06/29/2021

When the winds of change come blowing
As they surely will
May the gusts blow soft and warm
Gently on your skin
May your soul be firmly sown
With the seeds of bravery
And may your journey be illuminated
By your own strong energy

Fate

Willow struggled to fill her lungs with the heavy air that reeked with the ancient smell of age and the centuries that have already passed away. The trees that surrounded her small body rose from the tangled underbrush, creating a veil of secrecy, mystery, and shelter in this peculiar woodland known as the Crooked Forest.

The Crooked Forest makes you feel as though you have stumbled into a strange and spellbinding fairy tale. It is a place between places, not quite a part of the world that we know but rather a world that lies alongside our world, separated only by a crossroad. Here, the pine trees flourish and grow fantastically large, twisted at the roots with a curve-shaped arch near the base. Lifetimes before, when the trees were just young sprouts, a blizzard descended, freezing the young trees into a bent-over position. The snow weighed down the saplings as they were sprouting, causing them to grow crookedly.

Bracing herself against the base of a crooked pine tree for support, Willow placed one hand on her forehead and one hand on her heart. Feeling tightness in her chest and pounding in her temple, she closed her eyes tightly until the dizziness passed.

The center of her heart felt as though it had been deeply bruised. Willow was unaware that she was suffering from broken heart syndrome, a condition that could be brought on by receiving a sudden shock, emotional trauma, or bad news.

Fear and panic were taking hold of Willow's tiny body. Her knees began to quiver and shake, and she felt that she could no longer stand upright. Sliding her spine down the trunk of the tree until she was sitting firmly on the ground, Willow clasped her small hands over her eyes as the tears began to stream down her flushed cheeks, and time seemed to stand perfectly still. The realization that she had become separated from her dear mother and that she was now hopelessly alone had set in.

Where Willow sat sobbing, the timothy grass surrounding her now seemed to be more brown than green and the nearby flowers seemed to wilt and shrink as if they felt her great despair. Overhead, the tassel-eared Abert squirrel halted his playful antics and watched in pained silence as the little girl who was so deeply connected to nature mourned her devastating loss. It was as if all of Mother Nature's creations could feel the pain of Willow's broken heart. When the sobbing ceased and the tears dried, many hours had passed, and dusk was rapidly approaching. Little Willow had no more tears to cry, but the bruised feeling in her heart lingered.

A light evening breeze rustled the tall, thick blades of timothy grass. The soothing sound quieted the tiny girl's mind, as the warm air dried her tearstained face. Willow blinked twice, thinking she saw movement within the lush field of swaying grass.

As Willow stood to investigate, the grass where she had been sitting unexpectedly turned green and the nearby wilted flowers stood straight as an arrow. The Abert squirrel began to run overhead once again, as somehow nature sensed that Willow's distress had momentarily subsided. The air felt lighter, and the wind smelled sweeter.

Unexpectedly, the tall blades of timothy grass parted, and he majestically appeared. He remained stock-still, his deep brown eyes staring steadfastly into Willow's eyes. Striking a muscular and sturdy poise, the puppy carefully approached Willow, lowering his head to the ground as if bowing before lying down at Willow's feet, pressing his nose ever so softly against her tiny hand. Willow reached out to stroke the soft fur of this new visitor, and when she did, she felt a slight lift in her broken heart.

"My name is Willow. My mother named me this because it means 'strong and resilient' like a willow tree, able to withstand the strongest of storms. But after today's storm, I am not feeling so strong." Willow's voice trembled. "Do you have a name?" she questioned the inquisitive, intelligent, tricolored creature who was looking her steadily in the eye.

The little dog shook his head from side to side. Willow giggled at the sound of his big flapping ears.

"I will take that as a no." Willow smiled.

The puppy lowered his front legs to the ground as if he were going to playfully pounce before releasing a single shrill, high-pitched bark.

"Do you have a home nearby?" Willow inquired.

The puppy rolled over onto his back, raising all four paws into the air as he squirmed along the soft green grass that felt so good against his fur.

Willow looked in all directions, wondering where this splendid creature had come from. But there was no one else around. They were completely alone. It was as if he had mysteriously materialized out of thin air.

"You are most welcome to stay with me. That is, if you have no other place to be. I have the most delightful name for you," Willow continued. "I will call you Gyzmo. Do you know what that name means?" she questioned.

The puppy looked thoughtfully at Willow with his soulful, unblinking big brown eyes, cocking his head sideways as if processing her words.

"It means 'strong and handsome and always fighting for the greater good,'" Willow declared.

As the darkness of the night fell upon the sweet pair, Willow snuggled up next to her new friend, burying her face in his soft fur. As the hours passed, the two fell into a deep slumber lying side by side. As Willow curled up closer to Gyzmo, the tension in her body subsided, and her mind floated into a deep dream state, remembering back to how this difficult day had begun.

"Wake up, Mama!" Willow playfully nudged her sleeping mother. "You said we could gather mistletoe from the forest today."

Luna smiled lovingly at her cherished daughter as she rose from her bed and prepared a quick breakfast of berries and nuts for them both before they set out to gather mistletoe from the pine trees that grew thick within the Crooked Forest.

Willow and Luna were Shuns. The little people known as the Shuns were appropriately named because they had been shunned by human society for their deep reverence for nature and earth. It had come to pass that the humans had become disconnected from nature as they moved out of the forest and built communities nearby one another and formed towns. They had lost their sense of mystery and respect for something greater than themselves. Gone was their inherent connection for the celebrations associated with the cycles of the seasons that had previously been marked by festivals. Moving away from the closeness of the earth and into huts and cottages, the humans felt they had found a better way to live and had become intolerant of their former style of living and intolerant of the Shuns.

As the peaceful Shuns clung to their beliefs about nature's magic, they were criticized by the humans and labeled as country dwellers for their special kinship with Mother Earth. Known as keepers of the forest, the Shuns understood the connection between the land, the water, and the animals. They revered the tall ones commonly called trees and the old ones known as mountains. The Shuns understood that a single blessing could affect the next seven generations, so they lived with grace and ease, deriving joy in the simplest things—a single flower, the fragrance of freshly gathered herbs, and the constant movement of the clouds.

The Shuns had no need for a centralized government. They were bound by culture and belief. They had no written language and chose to pass on their sacred teachings orally and live by example. The Shuns stood only six inches tall and made their homes within the tall ones, inside the hollowed-out tree holes in the forest where they felt safe and protected.

Once, humans and Shuns lived side by side, sharing all Mother Earth provided. But now the humans wanted little to do with the Shuns and preferred to live nowhere near them.

On this morning, Luna and Willow had set out to gather herbs, in particular, mistletoe, which was revered for its curative properties. The Shuns knew that when gathering mistletoe, you should never let it fall to the ground. Mistletoe's magical properties are preserved by the fact that it lives suspended between heaven and earth.

Luna's quick, nimble fingers harvested the berries, leaves, and stems from the mistletoe plant that she would later boil into a medicinal tea and secretly consume to soothe the headaches that she was suffering from. Harvesting and consuming herbs was now strictly forbidden as it broke the new social rules put into place by the humans, forcing the Shuns to hide their practices from human eyes and human judgment to avoid persecution.

So when the human sheep herder named Aidan saw Luna gathering mistletoe within the Crooked Forest, he sneered and became irritated and annoyed as he had turned a deaf ear and a cold shoulder to the belief in nature's magic. Not only was Luna violating the law by gathering herbs, but her very presence also made her a witness to the crime he was preparing to commit against nature.

It seemed that Aidan had manifested a magnificent scheme to steal water from Sleeping Creek for Flowerville, the village where he lived. Flowerville had recently grown into record numbers, as the humans had moved far away from the forest and from Sleeping Creek. More humans in the village equated to more water consumption. Presently, Dragonfly Ditch was the only source of water that Flowerville had, and it was not considered to be enough. Aidan felt that if he could divert the water from Sleeping Creek by constructing a ditch, then those waters could be channeled and navigated into DragonFly Ditch, and Flowerville would have ample water.

Unaware of Aidan's watchful eyes, Luna paused in her gathering, sensing a shift in the weather as the wind began to pick up and black clouds darkened the sky. As she watched the sky change and the clouds shift, she felt a chill unexpectedly run up her spine, and she began to feel uneasy. Luna turned to check on Willow, who was softly singing a lullaby to her doll made from broomcorn.

Luna lovingly smiled at her daughter as she felt the vibration of the distant thunder in her bare feet, and blue lightning flashed in the sky.

"Whatever does that little Shun think she is doing? She knows that gathering herbs is strictly prohibited by the law!" Aidan said with no one nearby to hear him other than himself. "And furthermore, I am not going to allow her to interfere with my plan!" he grumbled, and his frown lines deepened.

Reaching into his pocket, Aidan pulled out a handful of stones and began hurling them at Luna. Luna was a ridiculously small target though since she stood only six inches tall, so the stones that sailed through the air missed her entirely. As the lightning flashed and the raindrops began to fall to the ground with a fury, Luna ran faster, dropping her basket of mistletoe and fleeing into the forest, becoming separated from Willow, who was still silently watching, clutching her doll to her heart.

Willow was paralyzed with fear and could not find her voice to call out, which was a blessing, as Aidan remained unaware of her presence. Suddenly, Willow felt a sharp pain in her heart as panic ensued, and her breath became short and ragged. The robust wind blew, and the sky darkened. Willow remained stranded and abandoned with only her broomcorn doll to give her comfort.

Luna had been running from Aidan for what seemed like an eternity. Stopping to catch her breath, she crawled inside a nearby tree hole, seeking safety inside the tall one. Burrowing down into the darkness of the cozy tree hole, a memory arose from a time not so long ago.

Ceri

Willow had never met her father, her mother being her only parent and the one who provided for her and met her daily needs. They say you cannot miss what you do not know, and Willow supposed that was true, although she was still curious about her father's absence nevertheless.

Willow's mother was named Luna, which meant "moon," and her birth father was named Ceri, which meant "beloved." Ceri was guarded closely by his large Shun family. His parents and siblings treasured their beloved son and brother so much that they secretly hoped to hold him tightly within their close-knit family circle forever. In their family, the blood bonds were thick and sturdy, leaving no room for an outsider to join their family unit.

Ceri's family considered him unavailable to be in any type of relationship that might jeopardize the loss they would feel if Ceri had truly left home and made a life of his own. His siblings required his presence and were reliant on him to entertain them, in what most of the world would consider an unnatural way. His family became irritated and jealous when Ceri and Luna spent time together. Sharing Ceri with Luna incensed the family, and they voiced their disdain loudly, hoping to strike discord within the couple's young relationship.

The family's arrogance was so strong that Ceri could not rail against it. He did not possess the strength required to speak up for himself. The truth was that it stoked his ego to be put upon such a high pedestal, and he relished the abnormal adoration that he received from his family. So Ceri did nothing. Doing nothing was far easier for him and remained a pattern throughout his life when it came to resolving life's difficult challenges.

"We could make a beautiful life together, Ceri," Luna lovingly said. "A life we could call our own, in our very own space, if only you can find it in your heart to begin a life with me."

But Ceri could not find his voice and remained silent, feeling a lump in his throat that prevented him from speaking.

Feeling like an unnecessary nuisance and an obtrusion, Luna never stood a chance. It didn't take long for her to realize that she was coming between the family household and their beloved Ceri.

So Luna left Ceri's company, knowing that she could never truly hold his heart, and Ceri remained unpartnered, even into old age, never having the courage to live his own unique life.

Feeling crushed and confused, Luna fled into the deepest recesses of the Crooked Forest, leaving Ceri and his strange and peculiar family behind. Soon thereafter, she felt the first sensation of the new life that was expanding inside of her. Listening to her instinct, Luna sought out a field of sprawling ivy that represented rebirth and regeneration and remained there for several months.

On the night of Willow's birth, Luna held her cherished infant up to the light of Grandmother Moon, asking her to hold Willow's heart closely, as well as all her hopes and dreams.

As Willow grew, Luna taught her daughter about the cycles of the moon as it waxes and wanes and how to apply those same principles to their life in the Crooked Forest. She taught Willow to rejoice in the brightness of the full moon, to experience the darkness and silence of no moon, and how to set her intentions with the dawning of the new moon.

Grandfather Sun warmed Willow and nourished her life as she grew from a baby to a young girl. Luna taught Willow that the stars in the sky held her own dear parents, Willow's grandparents, now long gone from their life on earth. But just like the night stars that allude sight during daylight, Willow's grandparents were still there, just like the stars, watching over Luna and Willow as they lived their lives in the beautiful, mystical Crooked Forest, where all things were possible.

Gyzmo was born into his earth life as a Pembroke Welsh corgi, a high-energy breed, meaning "dog of the dwarfs." His dog ancestors had been known to be great helpers of the Shuns. Legends spoke of how the dogs pulled the carriages and carts of the Shuns, providing them with transportation. They were considered as an enchanted dog of the fairy folk, and you need only to see a Pembroke Welsh corgi in the moonlight to know this is true. Willow had known that Gyzmo was special from their very first meeting. It did not take long for the pair to weave a special bond based on trust, companionship, and love.

Gyzmo had a thick double coat and a naturally darker patch of fur under his shoulder, commonly called a fairy saddle. But his beloved Willow wanted him to have something even more superior than the fairy saddle he was born with.

Distracting her aching heart from the broken heart syndrome she was suffering from, she gathered flowers from the forest, braiding columbine and lavender together to form a seat where she could ride upon Gyzmo's back. She interlaced ferns and coyote willow into a halter that she gently placed over his head so she could hold on tight as together they rode through the whimsical landscape of the Crooked Forest, discovering the magic of each new day and strengthening their bond.

As Gyzmo and Willow grew closer, Willow listened to his guidance more and more. Willow had been raised by Luna to believe that everything in nature was alive and that animals were our brothers and sisters. She trusted Gyzmo completely and considered him her salvation in an otherwise desperate situation.

"Are you feeling any better today?" Gyzmo would gently question his companion every morning when they woke.

"I don't know how to feel better." Willow sadly sighed. "I try, but each day feels just like the day before. Maybe I'm just not strong enough to feel differently."

Gyzmo was beginning to worry that Willow might never recover from the loss of Luna. He sensed the heaviness of Willow's grief, and he longed for her to heal. "True strength doesn't come from your physical body, Willow, but from the inner strength you naturally possess," Gyzmo gently advised. "Tomorrow is a brand-new day, and we have much to do," Gyzmo kindly whispered to Willow each night as they prepared for rest. "Sleep well tonight knowing that you are protected and held by the universe. Everything will look brighter in the morning."

That night, Gyzmo had a very distinct dream, and in his dream, he saw a brilliant patch of blue flowers near the headwaters of Sleeping Creek. Instinctively he knew that the water contained healing properties due to the presence of certain minerals. His dream told him that Willow needed these curative waters to heal. Drinking the sacred water would provide a physical cure for the broken heart syndrome that ailed her.

Gyzmo woke with a clarity knowing exactly what he must do to benefit his beloved Willow. His dream had revealed a message. It would take several days to locate the headwaters of Sleeping Creek, but Gyzmo knew that he must take Willow there.

Dewdrop

Dewdrop, the water fairy, gazed steadily at the reflection that mirrored back to her through the calm waters of Sleeping Creek. Pearly white skin framed her long blue braids and bright blue eyes. Sticking one elegant, webbed finger into the water, she was aware of the gentle ripple she had created, knowing that all her actions caused a similar type of reaction throughout the universe. She could breathe both water and air and could live in water or on land. She was the elemental guardian who resided at the headwaters of Sleeping Creek.

Dewdrop saw little that she considered an obstacle. She understood that her fate rested in her own hands. If Dewdrop could not flow through something, she would simply flow around it, choosing the path of least resistance.

From the depths of the crystal clear water, she pulled out a heart-shaped holey stone. Holey stones have a natural hole in them formed by water flowing through. They are considered magical and are used for protection and for healing. You do not find a holey stone. The holey stone will find you. Closing one eye, she peered through the hole in the stone and into the kingdom of the fae. Smiling to herself, she clearly saw the elementals of the fairy world dancing in the morning mist.

With webbed fingers, she carefully gathered the morning dew from the nearby columbine flowers and gently poured dewdrops through the opening in the stone, connecting the holey stone to the fairy spirits and the one whom the stone was meant for. The gift of the holey stone would grant the bearer a shield of protection. It would not be long now. She knew that his arrival was imminent.

A New Beginning

Gyzmo woke knowing that today was the day. He gently nudged Willow's hand with his nose, waking the tiny girl from her slumber. "Willow, wake up! There is someplace special I want to take you!"

But Willow was not immediately receptive. Like a flower that yearned for the sunlight, Willow yearned for Luna. Reaching out her tiny hand, Willow stroked the fur on Gyzmo's head. Gyzmo lowered his head nearly to the ground as her fingers met his fur, a habit he had from their very first meeting. A single tear fell down Willow's cheek. Her heartbreak had left her feeling turned inside out. Willow's fear of being forever alone had been eased by Gyzmo's company, but she had no idea that Gyzmo had been a blessing sent to her from the fairies to aid in the healing of her broken heart.

"You will need to go through the pain, not around it," Gyzmo gently whispered to Willow as she stroked his fur on the morning of their departure. "Stand still and feel the crack in your heart, little one," he wisely continued. "This is the way you will mend the pain you are feeling."

"How can I ever forget that horrific scene and the day that changed my life forever when that horrible, awful human hurled rocks at my mother?" Willow questioned.

"When you find it in your heart to forgive him, your great sadness will evaporate. You must move past your anger and fear and find forgiveness, Willow. It is then that your burned and bruised heart will heal, and you will be able to move forward toward your destiny and the life that you were meant to live." Gyzmo gently placed his round white paw over Willow's tiny fingers. "I'm here to help you every step of the way, Willow," Gyzmo sweetly spoke.

Glancing down at the kind gesture Gyzmo offered, Willow's heart was touched, and she knew that she must try, even though her true inner strength eluded her.

"We are destined to be together, Willow. Our meeting had nothing to do with coincidence and everything to do with fate," Gyzmo continued genuinely. "There is a place that I am destined to show you. Will you go with me?" Gyzmo asked.

"I will go with you, Gyzmo," Willow quietly spoke as she placed the fairy saddle onto the tiny dog's back and gathered the flower reins of the halter in her hands. Preparing for departure, she climbed bravely upon the saddle onto the young dog's back as the bright rays of sunshine shone down upon the pair, as if guiding them on their journey and sealing the fulfillment of the fairy blessing in the warm beams of glowing sunlight.

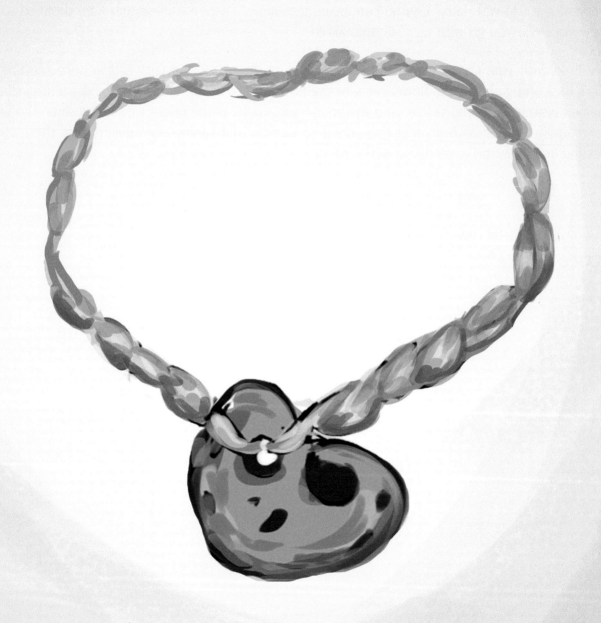

Gyzmo recognized that they had reached their destination. This place looked exactly like his dream. A field of forget-me-nots carpeted the moist meadow ahead. The blue flowers with yellow centers and green leaves that resembled mouse ears were abundant. Folklore spoke of forget-me-nots being worn or carried to ensure that the bearer would never forget the one they were thinking of.

Gyzmo promptly picked a flower and presented it to Willow.

"For you, precious Willow. May you never forget your dear mother, Luna, and may you keep her close to your heart until you two shall meet again."

"How kind of you," Willow said as she graciously received the flower, tucking it next to her heart for safekeeping.

Bumblebee and butterfly wings murmured in the air. The rich nectar of the woodland flowers hung heavily as the audible rhythmic gurgling sound of water indicated that the pair had reached their desired destination.

"It's magnificent here!" Willow whispered in awe of the staggering beauty that she was surrounded by.

Unexpectedly, a buzzing noise like that of an insect could be faintly heard overhead. Gyzmo looked up to see a small being with glistening blue wings circling his head. The creature was dazzling in color, the size of a firefly.

"I am Dewdrop, the elemental fairy and guardian and protector of Sleeping Creek. I have been waiting for you," Dewdrop quietly announced.

Gyzmo began to gently sniff the winged one who had settled herself directly upon his nose.

"I am pleased to meet you Dewdrop." Gyzmo smiled. "This is my companion, Willow. I have brought her here as I was instructed to do in my dream."

"I am so glad you have safely arrived, dear ones." In an instant, Dewdrop flew away, immediately returning, holding a beautiful necklace in her tiny blue hands.

"This is Mother Earth's gift to you, Gyzmo. It was your destiny to make this journey. I present to you this heart-shaped pendant. It is called a holey stone. This holey stone holds the power of the fairy kingdom. From the petals of fairy slippers, I have woven this necklace chain to hold the holey stone in place."

"For me?" Gyzmo asked, choking back tears.

"For you, Gyzmo," Dewdrop whispered, flying over him and ever so gently dropping the necklace down and over his head. "Mother Earth wants you to know that you are appreciated for your kind heart and for your endeavors to heal Willow from her broken heart syndrome. As the protector of Sleeping Creek, it is my duty to bestow this holey stone to you, which will grant you protection for the rest of your days."

Gyzmo's dream had not revealed that he was to receive a gift, only that he was to bring Willow to this place. He was awestruck by the gifting of the holey stone, and his heart swelled with pride and gratitude as he was presented the magical talisman.

"Why, thank you, Dewdrop," Gyzmo spoke as he sat proudly, wearing his new necklace.

Dewdrop fluttered her glistening wings as she looked lovingly down at Gyzmo. "Thank you, Gyzmo, for making a positive and caring difference in the world."

Dewdrop reached out to pet Gyzmo, and the puppy lowered his head to the ground as he always did when he was stroked.

"You are a true gentleman bowing in that very noble way. With the powers of the fairy world, I knight you and rename you Sir Gyzmo," Dewdrop said, lightly touching his right and left shoulders with her fairy wand. "Your honorable character must be rewarded. I pronounce you Sir Gyzmo, the Pembroke Welsh corgi."

Dewdrop momentarily disappeared only to instantaneously reappear, carrying a tiny pouch filled with the magical water of Sleeping Creek.

"Willow, you are to drink this water to aid in the healing of your broken heart," Dewdrop advised as she handed the pouch to Willow.

Willow was speechless as she accepted the precious gift from the blue creature.

"I also have a message meant for you, Willow," Dewdrop continued.

Willow could not have been more surprised. "A message for me?"

"The universe understands that you have a question, dear girl. It is my duty to tell you that the one who holds the answer to the question that is in your heart is nearby, and it is the perfect time for you and Sir Gyzmo to meet her."

"Meet her? Where?" Willow questioned.

"She lives at the end of a narrow, winding road, well-worn by worried folk who have lost something or are at their wits' end with a personal problem. She is known as the Mystery Woman of the Hills."

"However will we find her?" Willow anxiously questioned.

"You will travel to Rushing River. There, you will see a mile-long road that you will follow to a clearing. In the clearing, you will see an apple orchard and a two-room log cabin. Disturb nothing on this land as you pass through. The Mystery Woman insists that nothing on her land be killed, not even a snake. She refuses to have any timber cut from this land, and she heats her cabin only from the trees that are already dead or dying. The land is considered sacred."

"How will I recognize her?" Willow questioned.

"She possesses light-blue eyes and honey-colored hair. She is greatly respected, and her personal needs are minimal. She belongs to a race of humans who can 'see.' She resists being called a fortune-teller, and she will not accept compensation from you for her services. She uses her power for only good and delights in greeting her visitors with the answer to their question before they can even ask."

"Will she know where my mother is?" Willow questioned, feeling her heart begin to race with anticipation.

"That is not for me to know. I must leave you now, dear ones," Dewdrop answered.

"Wait! Can you direct us on which way to go?" Sir Gyzmo excitedly inquired.

Dewdrop pointed her elegant, webbed finger. "This way. Rushing River emerges from a roaring, fathomless spring, thus its name. Speculation as to the true depth of the spring has circulated for centuries and has grown into legends. The bottom of the spring has never been fully realized. Look to the north when you find the spring, and the road to the Mystery Woman's cabin will be visible. Blessings to you, dear ones, and safe travels." And in the blink of a fairy's eye, Dewdrop vanished, leaving Sir Gyzmo and Willow alone at the headwaters of Sleeping Creek.

When our hearts are broken
We sometimes lose our way
Yielding to emotion
And disengaging from our days
But hope can spring eternal
From our power deep within
Gifting us the strength
To aspire once again

Intentions

Sir Gyzmo and Willow gazed in the direction Dewdrop had directed them, still feeling slightly dazed from their encounter with the elemental water fairy.

Willow closed her eyes and drank from her sacred water pouch, remembering how Luna had taught her how to set her intentions and voice them to the universe.

"May my great sadness be lifted, no longer able to hinder me or hold me prisoner. May any feelings that no longer serve my greater good fall away from me like the dying petals of a rose."

As the sacred water poured through Willow's small body, she felt a warmth run through her veins and she sensed the birth of her inner strength. She acknowledged that life would include highlights of happiness and joy, as well as low lights of despair. To expect more was futile and frankly a waste of her time. Putting one tiny foot in front of the other, she took the first steps into her new life. It felt frightening and exhilarating all at the same time.

Her expectations of a perfect world containing Luna was not to be. At least for now. But no longer could she drown in the depths of her great sadness. Instead, she would move forward, setting her mind and her intentions, vowing to live in the now and relish the great mystery that the future holds.

Sir Gyzmo smiled his precious corgi smile at his beloved Willow knowing that he had done the right thing by bringing her to the sacred headwaters of Sleeping Creek. He sat tall and proud, wearing his holey stone necklace and knowing that he had made a difference in the world.

When Willow opened her eyes, they were filled with gratitude and hope, and she felt a lift in the weight that she had carried on her shoulders as she gave her worries up to the universe by setting her intentions.

"You look striking wearing your holey stone, Sir Gyzmo."

Sir Gyzmo felt taller, and his chest felt broader as he happily displayed the magical talisman that covered his chest.

"Are you ready for our next adventure, Willow?" he softly inquired.

"I am!" Willow pronounced confidently. And with that, the journey to locate the Mystery Woman of the Hills began.

The Mystery Woman

The Mystery Woman of the Hills had been living alone upon her mountain overlooking the headwaters of Rushing River for over fifty years. She had inherited her sixth sense from her grandfather. "My grandfather was the greatest seer in the land, and that ability was handed down to me. I must find a way to do virtuous things with this gift," she was known to say.

As a younger woman, she had been a caregiver but had not stayed with it as she could not stand the strain of knowing what was going to happen to those whom she cared for. As she aged, she knew that it was her destiny to live alone and remain unmarried. "What husband would want a wife who knew his every secret and thought?" she said knowingly.

As dusk approached on the mountain, the Mystery Woman settled her old bones in her ancient rocking chair that creaked each time she rocked. In her lap, she held her healing bundle. Ever so gently she untied the strings of braided yarn that held the pouch in place and viewed the contents that contained the teachings from other beings who had transferred their power to her.

Inside was an assortment of feathers, cedar, sage, and sweetgrass, along with her medicine pipe and tobacco. She tamped the tobacco into the pipe and lit it carefully. She relaxed as she drew the smoke into her lungs. Exhaling, she blew two whiffs of smoke toward the heavens and two whiffs toward the earth.

From the bundle, she took out a whistle. Two days ago, she had gathered wild rhubarb from the Crooked Forest and carefully roasted the stalks. Using her pocketknife, she had carved a whistle from the rhubarb stalks. She held the whistle in her long-worn fingers, turning it over to examine the craftsmanship. It was exquisite.

Closing her eyes, she focused her mind, and she began to see. She often told others how her powers worked. "It's like walking down a road. I can see quite a distance behind me and quite a distance ahead, but far away, things begin to get dim in every direction." Her wrinkled eyelids remained closed as she gently rubbed the whistle with her fingers. The vision was clear now. They were close.

The Visit

The rickety door of the old cabin creaked and groaned as it swung open, and a slight ancient woman appeared, her silhouette framed by the sunlight and the glistening spiderwebs that clung to the doorframe.

"She's alive!" were the welcoming words that Sir Gyzmo and Willow received from the Mystery Woman. It was as if her cool, unblinking light-blue eyes looked right through them, making it difficult for them to maintain eye contact with her.

Sir Gyzmo and Willow stared at each other, their mouths falling open in shock. Dewdrop had predicted that the Mystery Woman would assuredly answer their question before they could ask.

"Come inside?" the Mystery Woman inquired, moving from the open doorway so that they could enter. The modest home had a well-worn kitchen table with two rickety chairs. In the corner was a single pallet on the floor used for sleeping. A woodstove in the corner offered some warmth in the otherwise cold, dank little home.

"Thank you." Willow finally found her voice. "I'm Willow, and this is my companion, Sir Gyzmo. We've been traveling for—"

"Three days," the Mystery Woman interjected. "I've been waiting for you."

"How did you know?" Willow gently questioned.

The Mystery Woman let out a chuckle. "I'm double-sighted, you know. I can see two worlds at the same time. I knew you were coming, and when you arrived, you would want to know if Luna was alive."

"That's correct," Willow responded.

"Sit!" the old woman commanded. "I'll fix you some tea." The Mystery Woman shuffled toward the woodstove, reaching for her teapot, placing the iron kettle on the hot burner. From her meager cupboard, she fetched two small teacups and a bowl that she filled with spring water, setting it gently at Sir Gyzmo's feet.

"Rest, little one. You have had a long journey," she spoke as she stroked Sir Gyzmo's soft black fur, and he lowered his head at her touch as all gentlemanly, knightly dogs would do.

The tea kettle whistled, signaling that the water had boiled. The old woman filled two teacups and set them on the table, as the smell of wintergreen tea wafted throughout the cabin.

Willow sipped her hot wintergreen tea before speaking. "Can you help me find her?" Willow asked.

The old Mystery Woman sipped her hot tea and closed her pale, wrinkled eyes. "I can. She is alive, and she misses you terribly, Willow. She is nearly as sad as you over this separation."

"How will I find her?" Willow's voice trembled.

"By studying the clouds. Clouds bring messages that tell an unfolding story. By discerning the cloud shapes and witnessing their evolution and shape change, you can foretell specific events and how they will come to pass, Willow. With practice, you will cross over to another level of consciousness where you will enter a magical plane, leaving behind your conscious mind. By studying the imagery in the clouds, you will gain insight. This will help you process the feelings that are going on inside you."

"But I know nothing of this," Willow argued. "I do not have the knowledge to know what to look for."

The old Mystery Woman set her teacup down on the table. "You will learn, my dear. The preferred clouds for reading are cumulus clouds. Light, puffy clouds will bring messages down from the heavens and will assist you in discerning the future."

"I don't know how!" Willow cried. "Or where to begin!"

"It's always best to start at the beginning." The Mystery Woman smiled. "Come."

Opening her front door, she directed Sir Gyzmo and Willow out into the sunlight.

"Take a deep breath, focus, and tell me what you see, Willow."

Willow looked up into the immense blue sky, settling her focus on a puffy orange cloud that seemed to stand out from all the others. "That one." Willow pointed her tiny finger at the orange cloud that was reflecting the sunlight.

"Orange clouds indicate unresolved emotion and suppressed anger," the old woman retorted. "That seems very fitting for what you are feeling at this current time. You are more attuned to reading clouds than you even know.

"I don't know about reading the clouds." Willow sobbed. "I just want to find my mother."

"Then it's time for you to begin looking for her," the Mystery Woman said. Reaching into her apron pocket, she retrieved the whistle she had carved from wild rhubarb and presented it to Willow. "I crafted this especially for you, Willow. You will instinctively know when it is time for you to use it."

The Mystery Woman's cool blue eyes fixed on Willow. "I can plainly see that you were born into this life to become a heroine, Willow." Turning her gaze toward Sir Gyzmo, she continued, "And you, Sir Gyzmo, will become a hero."

"You were both born with a destiny for greatness. Heroes and heroines do not sacrifice themselves for others, and they never go against the greater good. Going against your destiny will only prevent you from living into your whole potential. And even though it is wise for both of you to never forget a betrayal, it does not mean that you cannot find forgiveness for those who have betrayed you.

"Now off with the two of you! It is time to begin the search! There is a field of cloudberries growing in the meadow over that hill. Take a rest there, lie down, and relax upon the earth. Sample some of the delicious cloudberries. Their soft, juicy golden orange fruit is rich in vitamins and will assist you in building stamina. Look up at the clouds. See what you see. The answers to the questions you seek will begin to be clear at that time."

Cloudberries

Willow and Sir Gyzmo were in good spirits as they departed the cabin where the Mystery Woman of the Hills resided. The mysterious old woman had added hope to an otherwise hopeless situation by announcing that Luna was alive. If only they could find her.

Just a short distance from the cabin was a large lush green meadow. Jade-green plants had created an abundant ground cover, and the vines drooped with the plump, ripe weight of the elusive cloudberries that clung to them.

Willow squealed with delight at the discovery. "Look, Sir Gyzmo! Beautiful cloudberries!"

Sir Gyzmo approached the rare fruit plants, carefully sniffing each one as he was unsure of how they would taste since he had never encountered them before.

Willow popped a berry in her mouth and smiled. "The flavor is so unique. You simply have to try them to understand how delicious they are."

Sir Gyzmo smacked his lips as a bright-orange ring of berry juice covered his sweet face. "They are tart and sweet all at the same time," Sir Gyzmo announced.

"They will sustain us with the energy we will need in order to find my mother," Willow advised as she filled her pouch with cloudberries while simultaneously popping the delicious fruit into her mouth.

As they satisfied their hunger by feasting on the elusive cloudberries, Sir Gyzmo and Willow felt compelled to lie down in the lush meadow for a rest just as the Mystery Woman had said they should. Looking up into the sky, Willow felt herself relax as she began to study the clouds. But before she could discern any messages that the clouds might impart upon her, Willow and Sir Gyzmo fell into a deep sleep. The heat of the sun warmed their bodies, and they were satisfied and content with their bellies full, tucked away in their cozy resting place.

Aidan

Pulling a medium-sized pebble from his pocket, Aidan carefully placed the stone in the long, thin cradle of the shepherd's sling he had crafted from sheep wool. Holding the braided straps of the sling in his opposite hand, he aimed at the wayward sheep who had split from the herd. The stone landed at the sheep's foot, persuading the animal to rejoin the herd and move to the desired location.

Aidan's entire life had been centered around farming and raising sheep within the Crooked Forest. He knew that he was near the rare cloudberry patch and that it was exactly the right season to harvest the berries. As he approached the meadow where the cloudberries grew, he saw a tiny Shun girl lying on her back, studying the clouds. Beside her was a sleeping puppy with a talisman around his neck. The sight instantly irritated him.

He squinted his eyes in disdain as he peered through the fruit-laden bushes. "These Shuns don't ever seem to get the message that they are no longer welcome here." Aidan grimaced.

Willow woke with a feeling of being watched, and upon opening her eyes, she saw an ominous round black cloud directly above her, floating delicately across the sky. She immediately felt tension in her shoulders and neck as if something had gone wrong. Willow searched the sky for any messages, but the atmosphere only seemed to communicate gloominess as the black clouds swelled.

As Sir Gyzmo continued to snooze, Willow soundlessly rose from her sleeping place to stretch out her arms and legs.

"Don't you know you aren't welcome here?" Aidan roared in the direction of the small Shun.

Startled, Willow jumped and turned around to face a giant human man with a dark, weather-beaten appearance, who looked familiar.

"You were reading the clouds for signs, weren't you, girl?" Aidan questioned. "You know that cloud reading is against the law, don't you?"

Willow bravely straightened her small body to appear as tall as she could, but secretly her legs were trembling from fear and sudden surprise.

Aidan narrowed his eyes as he approached the tiny girl. "I know you!" he snorted in disgust. "You are the daughter of Luna. Like mother, like daughter, you don't seem to learn either. Your mother is the one I caught gathering herbs!"

"It's you!" Willow gasped, remembering the horrible man who changed the course of her life forever. "Why did you throw rocks at her and chase her?"

"She broke the law! Surely you know that practicing hocus pocus is strictly forbidden!" Aidan glared at the tiny girl.

"I am going to find her!" Willow cried with indignation. "And you can't stop me!"

Being mostly unfeeling, Aidan thought nothing of unleashing his unrestrained words. "She's dead, you know. No need for you to look for her in this life anymore. It is not until the next life that you will see her again. So you might as well make peace with what you cannot change."

Willow felt an oddly familiar pain in her heart as if it might be breaking in two all over again. She strained to process the words Aidan was hurling at her.

"Death is a transition, not an ending." Aidan craftily smiled. "You've had no ritual for her death, and that is why you can't accept the inevitable truth."

Willow felt as if her heart would explode and her tongue was tied. She simply could not find her voice to respond to Aidan's verbal assault.

"You need to put this idea of your mother being alive to bed once and for all. There is no way she could have survived in the forest after being chased for so long." Aidan was so close to Willow that she could feel his hot breath on her face as he spouted his rhetoric.

Willow's fingers automatically reached into her pocket as she located the whistle that the Mystery Woman of the Hills had carved for her from a rhubarb plant. Placing the whistle to her lips, she blew repeatedly with all the might her small body possessed until her savior appeared. Crashing through the underbrush, Sir Gyzmo gallantly emerged, his holey stone swinging as he ran. Willow jumped up unto Sir Gyzmo's back, firmly planting herself in the fairy saddle, while Sir Gyzmo charged ahead, saving his precious passenger from disaster and from the human who was intimidating her.

Crystal and Ember

Crystal, the Shun, had long blond hair and ice-blue eyes. She had been born in the Cave of the Crystals, and just like a clear quartz crystal, she possessed the energy of truth. She could not tell an untruth if her life depended on it. Telling a lie would run against her true nature of complete honesty and clarity. She was upbeat and positive, naturally repelling any negative energy she encountered.

Like the spark in a low burning fire, Ember, the Shun, possessed a quick and highly intelligent mind. Many underestimated his ambition due to his quiet nature. But his cool passiveness could turn into fire if he felt passionate about a matter. And if there was one thing Ember felt passionate about, it was Crystal. She was everything that he was not. Opposites in the expression of how they lived their lives, but nonetheless standing side by side at this time.

Sir Gyzmo had magnificently saved Willow from the troubling clash with Aidan by fleeing the cloudberry patch. Now the landscape began to transform, and the terrain became rocky and precarious as they entered a completely different region of the Crooked Forest. Sir Gyzmo stopped abruptly, nearly sending Willow airborne from her fairy saddle as he came to a halt directly in front of the tree hole that Crystal and Ember called home.

"Whoa there!" Ember cried, holding his hand in front of him so that the charging Pembroke Welsh corgi would stop before running directly over him and Crystal.

"What's the hurry?" Ember questioned as Sir Gyzmo breathlessly halted his stride inches in front of Ember.

"We have just fled from an angry and most disturbing human!" Sir Gyzmo replied.

Willow slid off her fairy saddle, her heart racing from the harrowing experience.

Crystal peered out of her tree hole home, surveying the scene with her quiet, calculating skills. "Are you both okay?" she asked.

"Yes, we are fine," Willow said breathlessly as she composed herself.

Crystal flashed a smile. "What happened? Why were you running from a human?"

"We are looking for my mother. She was chased into the forest by Aidan, who is the same human we were fleeing. I was told by the Mystery Woman of the Hills that my mother is alive and well, but Aidan was telling me something utterly different. He says she is dead, that she could never have survived his relentless pursuit and that I need to make peace with her death once and for all."

"Maybe we can help you with this predicament," Crystal replied sweetly. "I am Crystal, and this is Ember. We are happy to help you in any way that we can."

Willow smiled shyly. "I'm Willow, and this is my companion, Sir Gyzmo."

"Did your mother ever share with you the legends of the Cave of the Crystals, Willow?" Crystal inquired.

"No, not that I can remember. I don't have any idea where that even is," Willow responded.

"I was born in the Cave of the Crystals." Crystal smiled. "The cave is just over that knoll." She pointed.

"But why should we go there? What purpose would it serve?" Willow questioned.

"It is a holy place where vision quests are achieved. You just might be able to obtain some insight about your mother there. The Cave of the Crystals is a powerful place, Willow. If you decide to go, you must be prepared to have an experience you most likely will never forget. You will need to be brave. It is not a place for the faint of heart," Crystal wisely advised.

"The Cave of the Crystals is just over that knoll?" Sir Gyzmo inquired fearlessly, looking in the direction Crystal had indicated.

"I would take you myself," Ember answered. "But it would be wiser for you to travel alone. It sounds as if Aidan may be following you. Remember, you must always beware of the humans. You never know if they might be in an accommodating mood or not, unpredictable as they are."

Sir Gyzmo and Willow looked at each other knowing what they must do as Willow glided onto to Sir Gyzmo's back to prepare for their departure.

"Safe travels to you!" Crystal said kindly. "And good luck!

The Crooked Forest is a botanical mystery as old as the earth. Willow's fingers lingered on the twisted tree limbs that lovingly supported one another. There was a beauty in these silent sentinels known as the tall ones. It was as if they were guarding the secrets of nature.

There was a bright full moon that evening that illuminated the crooked pine trees, casting a bewildering magical spell so intoxicating that Willow felt light-headed and dizzy. She and Sir Gyzmo were standing underneath the powerful moonbeams that radiated down upon them.

"Are you frightened?" Sir Gyzmo asked Willow out of the blue.

"I feel calm, like this is something I have to do," Willow responded. "I feel as if my destiny is on the line. If I cannot live my destiny, then I will be working against my fate, and life will constantly be difficult. I must be brave and go inside the cave so I can find out if my mother is safe. If I know she is safe, then I think I can move toward the future."

"I want to go with you." Sir Gyzmo cried. "I want to be there if anything goes amiss."

"I have to go alone," Willow responded bravely. "But will you wait outside the entrance for me?"

"Of course, I will. If something feels odd or not quite right, you run out, and I will whisk you away from harm!" Sir Gyzmo responded.

Willow smiled lovingly at her faithful companion. "First, we have to find the cave."

It was as if the universe were listening quite intently and wanted to send them a sign, because at that precise moment, appearing in the dark forest was a trail shining brilliantly in the moonlight, as if inviting them into their future.

"This must be the way," Sir Gyzmo whispered. "Are you ready?"

Willow's fingers lingered on the tree branches that twisted, looped, and reached in every direction. "I am!" Her declaration sounded far braver than she felt.

Willow took the reins weaved from ferns and coyote willows into her small hands as she sailed onto Sir Gyzmo's back.

"We go!" Sir Gyzmo declared valiantly, as if he had made this ride numerous times in his young life. The sound of enchanted fairy bells began to chime, and a dash of fairy powder mystically steered Sir Gyzmo and Willow to the cave entrance.

Celestina stirred in her den, sensing she was being summoned. As the gatekeeper of the Cave of the Crystals, it was her responsibility to know if the traveler requesting passage was truly ready to enter.

Her long snout sniffed the air, utilizing her highly evolved sense of smell. Her powerful neck muscles flexed when she snorted as she stood up on her hind legs. She stood eleven feet tall and weighed over five hundred pounds. Her coarse, shaggy, cinnamon-colored fur glistened in contrast to the magnificent, gigantic selenite crystals she was surrounded by. This intelligent, soulful creature possessed the power of nine men but had the heart of a child.

Legend spoke of how Celestina, the heavenly cave bear, was nursed by the goddess of the Crooked Forest in a cradle that swung from bands of sunlight, between bent branches of budding crooked pine trees.

Celestina grunted as she slowly lumbered toward the cave entrance. Someone was waiting there for her.

The Cave of the Crystals

Willow and Sir Gyzmo arrived at the entrance effortlessly as if they had been steered by unseen forces. They had remained undetected as they arrived at the secretive entrance, which was mostly shielded from sight by a massive rock cliff overhang, rendering the hole in the mountain mysterious and rarely located.

"Be brave, Willow!" Sir Gyzmo whispered. "I'll be waiting for you."

Willow placed a kiss on Sir Gyzmo's furry forehead. "I will return as soon as possible." Without further ado, Willow made her way to the cave entrance before she lost her nerve.

Inside the cave, darkness was eternal, like an invisible force, and Willow felt the crush of blackness as if her very life could be squeezed right out of her. The distinct change in temperature was immediately apparent, as well as the cave's cold, damp, musty air.

Just a few steps inside, Willow froze, pressing herself against the cold, wet stone walls of the cave, her gaze skimming across the unyielding darkness. When her eyesight adjusted to the inky dark, she realized that she was surrounded by huge thirty-foot selenite crystals. Selenite is a calming stone that instills deep peace, clearing confusion, and aids with insight. The translucent white nature of selenite represents purity, light, and connection to the angel realm.

"Willow?" a voice in the dimness called.

"Yes, it's me," the small girl responded, her voice shaking ever so slightly.

Celestina, the cinnamon-colored cave bear, lumbered toward Willow. "I am here to help you with your quest, Willow."

Willow's eyes grew wide when she saw this fierce protector approach, but when she heard Celestina speak her name, Willow knew that she was safe from harm.

"Shall we go toward your destiny?" Celestina questioned.

"Yes, of course," Willow responded.

"The Cave of the Crystals is an entryway into another dimension that exists between realities," Celestina advised. "You are entering the goddess, and you will emerge into another world or alternate place."

Willow followed Celestina through several caverns and into the deepest recesses of the cave. Mysteriously, Willow's path seemed to be strewn with heart-shaped selenite crystals. Willow bent down to select a perfectly faceted white selenite crystal that glistened as she examined it while holding the stone in the palm of her hand. Suddenly, the heart-shaped gem cracked directly down the center, leaving the stone in two separate broken pieces. Willow was mesmerized and speechless, and she feared she was experiencing a hallucination.

"This crystal gem is broken, and your path is sprinkled with heart rocks, so I assume it is your heart that brings you to this place. Otherwise, the signs would indicate differently," Celestina wisely advised.

Willow held the broken heart rock gem in her hand as she listened carefully to Celestina's wise words.

"It is time to enter the dream lodge, Willow. I am the keeper of the dreamtime, and you are the dreamer. It is my responsibility to store the teachings until the dreamer wakes up to them. Are you fully awake and ready?"

"I am." Willow's voice quivered.

"In the dream lodge, you will find resolution to what troubles you. This will enable the healing to begin, and then you will be able to transform your goals into reality. You will eliminate that which is old, harmful, or useless. In the dream lodge, you will find your courage and strength. You will recharge your broken heart to begin anew," Celestina said as she vanished into the darkness, leaving Willow alone to prepare for her personal quest.

Willow created a sacred circle around her small body using four crystals, one to honor each of the four elements—earth, air, fire, and water—and placed one crystal on her stomach as she lay down within the circle. Closing her eyes, she drew in a deep breath to clear her mind of any lingering thoughts that could hamper her dream vision as she recited these words.

Mother Luna, come to me.
I call on you so that I can be
Confident, happy, and whole again
And find my strength that resides within.

"Connect with the source of life that guides and sustains when we are faced with life's darkness," she heard Celestina's faint voice murmur. Within moments, Willow drifted into a dream state, and her inner eye opened into a distant, foggy place that seemed familiar.

Fat, puffy white clouds dotted a turquoise-colored sky. She saw Luna gathering mistletoe from the crooked pines. It was as if Willow had journeyed outside her body, and she could see the scene unfolding before her. Luna suddenly turned toward where Willow sat playing with her broomcorn doll and flashed a brilliant smile at the daughter that she loved so much.

"Stay calm, precious girl. Feel the power of Mother Earth and the endless love she provides for you," Luna said. "You were born for greatness. It is your destiny to become a heroine. There is much to do, but you and your companion, Sir Gyzmo, are up to the task at hand," Luna said as the most beautiful silver wolf appeared at her side. Luna showed no fear of the mysterious creature. It was as if the two of them had known each other for a lifetime.

"Don't be afraid to travel in your life's intended direction. Be strong in your heroine's journey and know that I am safe and free of harm until we meet again," Luna whispered.

The wolf's golden eyes were unblinking as they peered through Willow's soul, but it was not frightening at all. One would think that the sudden appearance of a wolf would invoke fear. But this was not the case. A sense of calm and comfort flooded Willow's small body as the vision of the wolf and her dear mother already began to fade from sight.

The Awakening

Willow was not sure just how long she had been lying there as she fluttered open her eyes. Time, as she knew it, had stopped, and she felt tired and groggy as she struggled to sit up. Glancing around, she noted that she was all alone. Or was she? She had just seen Luna with the silver wolf so clearly, but they were not here now. Stepping outside the sacred space she had created for herself, she called out for Celestina. But the magical cave bear did not appear. Had Celestina simply been a figment of her imagination? As she steadied herself and gathered her bearings, she felt as if her mission were complete, and she turned to make her way back toward the cave entrance. She needed to find Sir Gyzmo. She had much to tell him.

When she reached the entrance, she hesitated for only a few seconds, feeling slightly fearful of leaving the dream lodge to return to reality. Looking behind her, she searched for Celestina, her vision quest guide. She would have loved to see her again and share the experience of her vision. But only the empty blackness presented itself. Celestina, Luna, and the silver wolf—none of them were there, and there was no reason to stay in the Cave of the Crystals any longer.

She squinted as she stepped into the bright sunlight just outside the cave entrance, as her eyes fought to adjust to the glare of the sun's rays as she emerged from the darkness.

"Willow?" she heard Sir Gyzmo's voice before she was fully able to focus upon his shape. "What happened?" he asked worriedly.

"Celestina, the cave bear, led me to the dream lodge and helped me prepare for my dream quest. I saw my mother, and a silver wolf accompanied her. I had never seen him before. Yet it was as if he had known my mother forever."

"What was said?" Sir Gyzmo inquired.

"That I was born for greatness to become a heroine and that I was sure to accomplish this task with your help," Willow replied. "Maybe I have reached a turning point," Willow continued wistfully. And at that exact moment, it appeared that Willow was experiencing a resetting of the inner compass that guided her, and she was flooded with the renewal of hope in her child's heart.

Suddenly, the fur on the back of Sir Gyzmo's neck raised as the sound of a snapping twig echoed through the air. Sir Gyzmo smelled him and felt him before he saw him. Aidan's dark eyes glowed with the fire of anger and resentment as he silently watched Sir Gyzmo and Willow standing at the cave entrance. Just as Crystal and Ember had predicted, they had been followed.

Before Sir Gyzmo had time to summon his heroine, she hopped onto his back and into her fairy saddle with the grace and ease of an experienced rider. The pair had no need for the exchange of words as their instincts were keen and their survival skills were sharp, as they instantaneously vanished in the blink of a fairy's eye, fleeing for safety.

Aidan was unable to react quickly enough to spoil the duo's escape. They had vanished. The sheep bleated in the distance, summoning Aidan back to his duties. He grumbled to himself, believing that Luna's daughter was causing just as much annoyance as her mother—practicing the old ways, living in the tall ones, gathering herbs, and staring into the clouds. He got angrier as he trudged toward his herd. Something had to be done to stop this nonsense.

Diversion

Two days had passed since Sir Gyzmo and Willow abruptly departed the entrance of the Cave of the Crystals after being spotted by Aidan. Only tiny rays of morning sunlight filtered through the denseness of the trees, lending a heaviness to the morning. Willow gazed at the gray clouds above her, sensing that something was amiss.

Abruptly Sir Gyzmo's big ears perked up as he strained to hear sounds in the distance. Willow glided off her fairy saddle effortlessly then crouched behind a columbine flower, surveying the disturbing scene unfolding before her.

It was Aidan. Armed with a pick and shovel, he was diligently digging a trench in the dirt alongside Sleeping Creek. He wore a profoundly serious expression, and sweat poured from his brow as he hit the hard earth time and time again with his pick.

"Just a little deeper." Aidan grimaced. "I will have this water diverted before you know it, and the villagers will think of me as a great magician!" He snickered. "I will be treated like a king by those peasants in Flowerville."

Aidan had not considered that his diversion plan would alter the flow of Sleeping Creek and compromise the only water source the forest creatures had. His strategy was to tell the villagers that he had willed the water to flow by simply asking Sleeping Creek to share its life source with Dragonfly Ditch. Flowerville would view him as a great and powerful magician, and he would be idolized by the villagers for solving the present water crisis. His mind returned to the memory of that annoying Shun called Willow and her equally annoying little dog that could practically fly, as if he were magic, sitting outside the Cave of the Crystals and talking nonsense about some vision the girl had. This remembrance irritated him and angered him.

Cunningly Aidan continued his mutilation of nature's perfect balance by driving his pick deeper into the ground, widening the trench. As the pick hit the earth, the water of Sleeping Creek broke through, and the diversion trench channeled the precious water into Dragonfly Ditch.

"I did it!" Aidan gleefully yelled.

Willow and Sir Gyzmo watched in horror from their hiding place. When the pick hit the earth and the water began to trickle through, Willow felt as if that pick had pierced her heart. She was deeply connected to Sleeping Creek after drinking from the healing waters, and she felt the pain that Aidan was inflicting.

Willow closed her eyes and steadied herself. She could not let this happen. "He must be stopped, and it must be now!" she stated softly.

Upon opening her eyes, she let out an audible gasp as she found herself locking eyes with the silver wolf from her vision quest. Silently they stared at each other as Willow realized that her mother's spirit animal had become her spirit animal as well. The wolf turned away from Willow to focus his gaze upon Aidan as he lowered his head while studying the human who believed he could manipulate nature.

Stealthily he approached Aidan, the pads of his great feet remaining silent atop the pine needles that covered the forest floor. Aidan's flock of sheep bleated and suddenly bolted, running into the forest. Aidan abruptly stopped his digging, sensing a predator, and finally, he saw the keen golden eyes peering at him through the crooked pine trees.

In that instant, the wolf communicated with Aidan. His sleek silver fur stood on end, and a deep growl rumbled from his massive chest. His yellow eyes locked with Aidan's eyes as he conveyed his disdain for the human's actions.

"Abundance, prosperity, and health are granted by the elemental world when one upholds the greater good. Tragedy can ensue due to the imbalance of a life lived in darkness and lies" was the message that was conveyed.

Events seemed to unfold all at once as the silver wolf shape-shifted into a stellar jay, noisily squawking, flying close to Aidan's face. Aidan threw down his pick and raised his arm to protect himself from the bird's fluttering wings as he clearly saw the warning of the disaster that was to come.

Willow felt altered from witnessing this profound experience. She was no longer the same child she once was. Something had shifted inside her, and she felt much older. She felt a connection to her mother through the silver wolf. It was as if the wolf were a bridge between mother and daughter. Through the wolf's eyes, she had seen the penalties and consequences of Aidan's actions, and it frightened her.

Willow saw that for as long as humans had been exerting their will upon the environment, the elemental world reacted. It seemed that water elementals could have an aggressive reaction to any attempt to change the natural course of the streams they guarded. In this case, Willow saw the beautiful blue creature named Dewdrop, who possessed the power to alter the weather and influence atmospheric conditions, and she saw the cost of Aidan's actions for himself and for Flowerville.

In the blink of a fairy's eye, Dragonfly Ditch dried up, leaving Flowerville stricken with drought, turning into a wasteland for the next seven generations to come. Prosperity and joy would no longer be found there, and life would become harder than it ever needed to be. The once lovely Flowerville was to become a pocket of stagnation where little energy flowed, rendering it a dead zone.

Aidan and his herd suffered as water was scarce, and greater distances had to be traversed to provide drinking water for himself and his sheep. In addition, he never had the opportunity to be known as a great and powerful magician since his diversion scheme was thwarted from the beginning.

If only Aidan had paid notice to nature's perfect balance, he might have reconsidered his destructive actions and worked toward an alternative solution that would have been of benefit to all creatures. But this was not to be. As it turned out, it became the dawning of an entirely new era for the humans in Flowerville—one where they felt the consequences of nature's power.

Redemption

Willow's life thus far resembled the gnarled and twisted branches of the Crooked Forest in which she lived, filled with bumps and snags along her journey. It was as if those crooked pine branches had held her prisoner, freezing her in their protective grip, where she remained captive, until just that very perfect moment in time when her heart healed and the branches thawed and released her from their icy grasp. That is when Willow summoned the courage to spring forward and grow into her full potential.

The grievous memories from that day in the forest when she became separated from Luna began to shift as Willow realized she could choose to remember the pleasant recollection of her mother's smile above the more distressing remembrance of their separation. That very circumstance that caused her such immense grief had turned out to be the very challenge that she needed to rise above to realize her destiny as a heroine.

As the folktales of Willow and Sir Gyzmo's adventures grew and spread throughout the woodland, other Shuns were moved to live their lives in the same manner, by being brave enough to search for their true destiny. There were those who would say "If Willow can do it, then so can I!" or "If Sir Gyzmo was that brave, then I can be brave as well!" Therefore, the greater good was realized throughout the land, and the Shuns prospered and thrived for the next seven generations to come.

When Willow closed her eyes, she could see her mother gathering mistletoe, and sometimes she felt the warmth of her mother's embrace just when she needed it most.

She thought back to her time spent in the dream lodge deep within the Cave of the Crystals. Her mother's presence was so real Willow believed that Luna was alive.

She gazed at the puffy white clouds drifting across the sky. These were the clouds that Willow saw and focused on the most these days. As Willow grew into a heroine, she learned that cumulus clouds signified that good fortune awaited just as she awaited the return of Luna and her own good fortune that would come to pass over time.

It was rumored that within the deepest recesses of the Crooked Forest, one could see a stunning fairy dog gliding effortlessly through the landscape. His saddle, made from columbine and lavender flowers, glistened in the sunlight as the halter, made from fern and coyote willows, rested in his precious passenger's tiny hand. It was as if the pair had been riding together throughout the centuries, suspended in time, in a place that ran just parallel of our current reality—a place and time that could be slipped into and out of at will, if one was trained and open to the ways of the mysterious, magical Crooked Forest.

Until we meet again . . .

Books by Joni Franks

The Corky Tails: Tales of a Tailless Dog Named Sagebrush book series

Corky Tails

Sagebrush Meets the Shuns

Sagebrush and the Smoke Jumper

Sagebrush and the Butterfly Creek Flood

Sagebrush and the Warm Spring Discovery

Rabos Taponados

Corky Tails Coloring Book

Sagebrush and the Disappearing Dark Sky

Printed in the United States
by Baker & Taylor Publisher Services